L. W Musick

The hermit of Siskiyou, or, Twice-old man

L. W Musick

The hermit of Siskiyou, or, Twice-old man

ISBN/EAN: 9783744749428

Printed in Europe, USA, Canada, Australia, Japan

Cover: Foto ©Andreas Hilbeck / pixelio.de

More available books at **www.hansebooks.com**

The Hermit of Siskiyou.

—OR—

Twice-Old Man.

A Story of the "Lost Cabin" Found, the
Fountain of Perpetual Youth
Revived etc.

By L. W. MUSICK.

Published from the office of the
Crescent City News.

Crescent City, Del Norte County,
California.

——1896.——

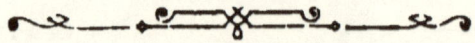

PREFACE.

The HERMIT OF SISKIYOU is designed (aside from the presentation of a readable story) to aid in the perpetuation of some of the quaint legends that have become in a degree historical of the region represented; and though the narrative is intended to be self-supporting, it is deemed but fairly consistent to offer therewith a more detailed statement of the accumulated evidences of its groundwork.

There is a distinctive grandeur and diversity of scenery within the Siskiyou range of mountains that affords to the bordering counties— Del Norte, Humboldt and Siskiyou, of northern California, and Josephine and Jackson, of southern Oregon—a background of wild and romantic splendor.

Snow crested and sun-girt, majestically stands the gray old dome, the sentinel of neighboring commonwealths and arbiter of their respective jurisdictions. Bluffly she casts her morning profile upon the western sea, and with greeting to the rising sun, her massive form substitutes the brief interval between the Sierra and Cascade ranges, as if to share with them the gravid burden of the great lakes thus pent of their anxious flow toward the Pacific and, as well, to assist in staying the border of the immense plateau that bears upon the easterly slope of this grand convention of mountain ranges.

Not alone upon her cragged exterior is the marvelous wealth of her wonders recognized and appreciated. Her immense caverns, of recent discovery, already rival in extent and magnificence the great Mammoth Cave of Kentucky, and will doubtless afford the scene of the world's greatest future subterranean exploration and development.

In some instances, where otherwise the subject matter might seem occult to any but the local reader, reference is made to an appendix, designed to supply such information. The first of these embraces a substantial claim for some place on Mount Siskiyou, or within its immediate surroundings, as the probable location of the world-famed "Lost Cabin." *

* See Note Two, Appendix.

If in any degree the "Hermit's Story" subserves the purpose of directing attention to the many deserving features of the district mainly presented, the patriotic endeavor of the writer will have been fully recompensed and his most extravegant hope realized.

Trustful of a generous forbearance, is respectfully subscribed

THE AUTHOR.

INDEX.

The Hermit of Siskiyou.

OR

Twice-Old Man.

A STORY OF THE "LOST CABIN" FOUND, THE
FOUNTAIN OF PERPETUAL YOUTH
REVIVED, ETC.

INTRODUCTION.

I.

THE setting sun was glint the breast
Of Mount Siskiyou, from whose crest
Was rifted on the scene below
Reflections of its virgin snow,
As cadence from Orphean harp,
Reverted from some cranny, sharp,
That floats in twilight's gentle glow
With measured accent, faint and slow.

And on the tops of giant trees,
Stirred lightly by the straying breeze,
A radiance as of burnished gold
Was clinging to each branch and fold;
While in the vale and canyon, deep,
The shades of night began to creep.

II.

Reposing in a pleasant glade,
Beneath the hemlock's ample shade,
A campfire's cheerful, ruddy ray
Consumed the waning light of day.
As if, in miniature, to gain
The conquest of Old Sol's domain.

III.

Prospectors were they who thus had made
The fire to burn within the glade;
And 'round its cheer-inspiring blaze,
With story of long by-gone days,
Discoursed they of each hopeful theme
Whereof, perchance, might lend a gleam
Of light upon a thing obscure;
Or, of some charm, the gods allure
And, peradventure, gain their heed
And counsel—then of great need.

IV.

Some busy were with all the ends
Of camp equipment, such as tends
To corporeal needs, when are required
As Pan or Morpheus have inspired.

V.

Yet one, of no such menial zest,
Seemed quite content himself to rest;
Save that his chin, with endless wag,
Was prone to chat, and even brag
Of what he knew of things, galore,
And what he'd heard long years before
Of treasure found and lost again—
And he, perhaps, the only man
Within the world's profound embrace
Who could divine its hiding place.

VI.

"Now, men," said he, "just hearken to
My candid words and counsel true:
Perhaps you're acquainted with
The story—some call it a myth—
Of how, in primal "days of gold,"
Was found a mine of wealth untold—
Upon the earth all scattered 'round—
And that the party who thus found
Did take thereof their hearts' content
And from the place forever went;
Nor has it been the lot of man
To gaze upon that spot again.

VII.

Yet while sojourning at the mine,
A hut they built, from logs of pine,
That in its fastness and alone
As the Lost Cabin still is known.

VIII.

Some think it quite remote from here,

Yet, (though to you it may seem queer,)
I'll tell you of a legend true
That claims it for Old Siskiyou;
As will, I trust, in time be found
Within the region here around.
And I would mrther say—but, hark!
A footstep! and the watchdog's bark!

IX.

Through mingled light of fire and sun
Was profiled on the horizon
A form so grand and marked of age
As reverence to at once engage
With great surprise and wonderment
Of whence he came—of what intent.

X.

Within decorous distance, he
Obeisance made, with courtesy;
And baring, then, his hoary head,
In voice sepulchral thus he said:

XI.

"Friends: If thus to you I may indite
My counsel, be ware of your plight!
Seek ye not in my domain
Aught of repose until you gain
Of one who, of a prior claim,
Hath preference and right to name
The conditions upon which you
May prospect on Old Siskiyou.

XII.

It is a fact I well divine

That you are seeking here a mine
Of wondrous wealth and ancient fame;
And of that goal seek I, the same.

XIII.

First, hear my story, then decide
'Twixt life and death; for woe-betide
Is he who seeks, without consent,
Upon these grounds to pitch his tent.

XIV.

Perhaps you've heard of Old French Hill—*
Of those in past, and even still,
Who're numbered with the dead or lost—
A region not remote, but crossed
By magic line, whereof is bound
The confines of enchanted ground.
Know ye! that of the past decade,
That from that lonely hill have strayed
Of hardy miners quite a score—
Nor will return for evermore.

XV.

I come not, though, with threat'ning rage;
But of true kindness, to presage
The evils that must fall in train,
And efforts that must prove quite vain,
Unless with purpose in accord
With charms within my knowledge stored,

---

* See Note Two, Appendix.

The Fates have willed it thus to be;
If not observed, doomed, then are ye.

XVI.

That you, each one, I may impress—
Lest of grave laws you should transgress—
Take ye from this faltering hand
This little stone—a talisman.
It will immunity assure
And from the Fates at once secure
The rights that they are wont to own
Inherent in this precious stone.

XVII.

Receive ye now the charm 'twill lend,
And from each one pass to your friend.
Thus will our friendship be made whole
And thus our efforts for the goal
Be rendered of account the best;
As will my story soon attest—
Related now, as best I can,
The memories of a twice-old man.

INTERLUDE.

THE red light of the pitch-pine fire
  Made ample cheer for all,
And around its radiant spire
  A distant sable wall;
Beneath whose seeming canopy
  Was spread upon the ground
A rude repast, of plenary,
  And all were gathered 'round.

WITHIN the circle, by request,
  And at the festal board,
The venerable and aged guest--
  Of friendship thus assured—
Began the story of his lives
  With all the amplitude
Of one who in earnest strives
  To be well understood.

THE HERMIT'S STORY.

———→ ● ◄———

I.

THE wondrous things I have in store
Date from a time long years before
All men, save I, now on the earth
Had knowledge of, or even birth.
Of fact, my youth and native place
Of consequence have no embrace;
Nor has my humble cognomen
Of great import that you should ken;
Save, that "Old Hermit," now applied,
May, of good fortune, soon deride
The one who thus denominates.
It is a caprice of the Fates
To change within the briefest time
The aged to their youth and prime.

II.

Then, if to me you deign to call,
I answer to the name of Paul;

But those who would of favor gain
Address me as "Sir Paul De Payne."

. III.

Of date my mem'ry serves me poor;
Though, of event, I am quite sure
'Twas while there raged most fearful strife
With brand and blade and scalping knife—
Yet known as King George's War—
From which I trace the fitful star
Thus far my wand'ring steps to guide—
With changing scene at every stride—
Till now I dwell within a cave,
Which threatens to become my grave;
There, sheltered from the winds and rain,
To bleach the bones of Paul De Payne.
Yet of the future's woe or weal,
Nor of the present, shall I deal;
Until my life from early date
I trace unto its present state.

IV.

Suffice it that my story tells
In briefest way, nor even dwells
Upon that one great theme of life—
The gaining of a faithful wife—
That briefly of it now I'll say:
She whom I loved was Lena Ray.

V.

Let bard and poet rhyme and sing

The rapturous theme, its charm, its sting,
And romance make of wondrous fame—
Whereof, included, ours the same.

VI.

I wooed to win, and winning, wed;
And by the stars now overhead
That radiate perpetually,
So judge ye of our constancy.

VII.

But sadly must I now relate
Of joys so brief and sorrows great;
For scarce one month had we been wed
When terror o'er the land was spread:
From Great Britain and old France—
From o'er the seas—did strife advance,
That grounded on colonial shore
With clash of arms and cannon's roar.

VIII.

And savage tribes with glowing brand,
With tomahawk and knife in hand—
With javelin and bended bow
And painted face of warlike show—
Did ally of the French pretend,
Though, as of foe, spared not the friend.

IX.

Of patience, and untiring hand,
Had I a home in Maryland,

Of rustic style and sculpture rude;
Hewn from the native forest wood.

X.

Of changing rule did I then stand
An alien, in my native land;
The subject of a regal crown—
Nor of its favor had renown.
And thus did I the more expose
Myself, than others, friends or foes,
To savage warfare and the torch,
Of which my flesh was made to scorch.

XI.

For soon there came upon the farm,
Within the night, the fire's alarm;
And as it cast its warning blaze,
Astonished, and with frenzied daze.
Was I taken from my bed,
And to a woodland near by led;
And pinioned was I to a tree
From whence I could not fail to see
The flames around our cottage burn;
Nor less the fearful sight discern
Of savages, with fiendish laugh,
Thrust in the flames my better-half.

XII.

And kindled at my feet had they
A fire that blazed with scorching ray;
Yet with their orgies 'round the fire,
That seemed to be a funeral pyre,

The wretches were the more intent,
And, of the time, from me they went;
When on a glowing window shined
A form angelic, pantomimed;
And ere the flames had lapped between,
Of farewell gesture had I seen.

XIII.

Then praying God to make me strong,
I surged against and broke the thong
That bound my arms around the tree;
Then loosed the others, and was FREE.
But, oh, the word—what mockery!
How undefined is liberty!

XIV.

Beyond the hope of human strife
Was it to save more than my life;
Nor of avail was it to stay,
Nor less of dread to run away.
Yet fear oft times the heart beguiles
With franticness or groundless wiles:
No joy behind nor hope ahead,
Into the darkness then I fled.

XV.

Through copse and glade and glen I went,
With scarce a purpose or intent—
Throughout the night and then the day—
Till reached the Monongahela;
Where Indian boat I found there moored,
Replete with all eqipments stored

For voyage of days, or weeks perhaps,
Consisting of provisions, traps,
Bows, arrows, gun and deadly spear;
Nor owner of did there appear.

XVI.

Of consequence you well may guess,
No scruples had I to possess
The ready craft, with its cargo,
And down the river swiftly row;
When on its winding way I steered—
Nor of its course cared I, nor feared;
But wildly onward was my theme
Heedless of whither went the stream.

XVII.

Not then, as now, was there extant
The knowledge of the late savant
Of books and charts that bear attest
Of wonders in the great wide-west;
Nor of the then existing lore
Had I of learning much in store;
And of the river's source and trend
I knew not whence, nor where 'twould end.
Grave night its sable cast had spread
Around, about and overhead;
And though from danger more secure,
Of spectre foes there were full more.

XVIII.

The bravest heart oft dreads the night

And from its phantoms takes affright,
And of the awe, inspiring show
Forgets the threat'ning real foe.

XIX.

The dense nocturnal atmosphere
Made gurgling stream with voice appear,
And e'en the firefly's tiny spark
A lamp light in the distant dark;
And when on light of real blaze
My eyes were fixed with wondering gaze,
It was with hope to meet with friend;
Though fears my longings would attend
Lest savage hands had made the fire
And savage hearts were lurking there.

XX.

Day had dawned, and with it came
Assurance more and scenes more tame;
But of account was it to make
Assurance sure, and thus to take
Within the day, ensconced, to sleep,
And through the night my wand'rings keep;
And suiting action to the thought,
My boat was then to anchor brought.

XXI.

Through interstice of drooping bough
With stealth I shoved my brave canoe,
Where, sheltered near the wooded bank,
Into deep slumber soon I sank,

And in my boat, as also, bed,
I slept as sleep the long-past dead;
And when awaked, it yet was day;
Though, of a truth I cannot say—
Nor ever will be ascertained—
If DAY, or DAYS, had intervened.

XXII.

The clear blue sky first met my gaze
Through emerald sheen of leafy haze,
With twig of elm tree interwove;
And birds there sang of joy and love.

XXIII.

All round me seemed a paradise,
With naught remiss of good device;
And though aroused to consciousness
Of what had been my grave distress,
And round my heart its horors crept,
I knew not if I swooned or slept.

XXIV.

Yet half persuaded to be glad
Then was I, of a vision had,
While as, perhaps, within a trance,
That gave to me foretelling glance
Of things not of the mind's accord—
Nor yet so vague as ought discard.

XXV.

And stirring, then, my vision seemed

As though I had but only dreamed;
Yet, still, within my secret mind,
The hope of something, undefined,
Gave strength of will and courage, bold,
To live the life in dream foretold.

XXVI.

Then came the time when sedate owl
Goes forth from nest, the woods to prowl;
And bat let loose from hanging perch
Sets forth upon his night's research;
And robber, from his secret den,
To slay and rob his fellowmen.
Though not of purpose as with them,
My boat I launched into the stream;
And once again within its fllow,
Sped onward, to the Ohio.

XXVII.

And now suffice it that, in brief,
I trace that stream to its relief
Within the Mississippi tide,
And of the then eventful ride
State, only, that succeeding days
Were fraught with all the stern amaze
That e'er adventure served to thrill
The song of bard or poet's quill.
And there where meet, with one assent,
The waters of a continent,
Rode I, at the dawn of day,
Upon its swift and turbid way.

"Father of Waters" was the name
That Indian tribes gave it, of fame,
And of the stream—its every branch—
Of sole dominion claimed the French.

XXVIII.

Then drifting down with will intent
To cross the stream ere far I went,
Of chance I met a small bateau
With Frenchmen at the helm and row.

XXIX.

Deliverance was at once assured,
And boat to boat then fast secured,
And story briefly told, I fell
Prostrate, and o'er me came a spell,
A dream or vision as before;
And seemed there from the splashing oar
To come a gentle, mellow voice
That bade my weary soul rejoice.

XXX.

The past and future, to my mind,
Were, with the present, then combined:
I saw cliff-dwellers on the shore,
And mound-builders, as of yore;
And, on the dark and turbid flow,
Forms bent o'er the dead De Soto;
And then, beneath the darkling wave,
Beheld De Soto's humid grave;
When, of a sudden changing sheen,
I met the maid Evangeline

Who once sought there, with hopeful spell,
Again to find her Gabriel.

XXXI.

And then, anon, I met a boat
That seemed a paradise, afloat,
With cloud-like vapor streaming back
And people crowded on her deck.

XXXII.

Great cities thronged on either shore—
And then there came a fearful war,
And iron boats were made to float;
And many things of wondrous note
Before me came while in my trance;
But great of all, I ween, per chance,
At least, within my own attest,
The voice that counseled me: "Go west."

XXXIII.

And when awakened from my dream
We many miles were up the stream,
And, halting by the wooded shore,
Our goods proceeded to unstore.

XXXIV.

And on the bank a village stood,
Where cast the shade of cottonwood
With sycamore and poplar tree,
And feathered choir of orchestra
Discoursed from lofty, sheltered bower

With melody to charm the hour,

XXXV

With cottages, a few, and rude,
And wigwams in disorder strewed,
The scene appeared distracted of
A primal trysting-place of love;
Though warm of heart were those who gave
To me of cheer and kindly lave;
And Indian rivaled with the white
Of merest whim to expedite,
Until decided was I to
Remain with them in friendship true.

XXXVI.

And parties forth were sent, afar,
To aid their allies in the war;
And deeds of horror to relate
Were reckoned of the war's estate—
When from the distant Orient
Came story of grave discontent·
That in a region far and strange—
And past the Alleghany range—
Had brave Choctaws gone forth to fight
And stormed a farm-house in the night,
And, "deed of valor" to proclaim,
A helpless woman cast in flame;
Though of a man, whom they had bound,
Escape had made, nor yet was found.

XXXVII.

Then came the soldiers of King George

And, of their vengefulness to gorge,
Pursued the braves, then in their flight,
Surprising them within the night
When they had halted near the shore
Where left their boat some days before—
Though when returned no boat appeared,
Which of escape then interfered.

XXXVIII.

Then swooped the soldiers of the Crown
And, without mercy, cut them down,
Save one who plunged into the tide
And crossed it to the other side,
And homeward with the news to tell
And dire revenge to stir, as well,
Sped onward as the fleeting roe
And fiercely as the buffalo.

XXXIX.

Then hurrying scenes of men and boats,
And piercing cries of warlike notes
Were on the earth and in the air
And life pervading everywhere;
And then the capering warrior dance
Of those equipped for its advance—
All painted and of frightful show
As if to scare away the foe.

XL.

And Frenchmen wondered with alarm
At signs portentious of great harm:

No longer in the war conclave
Were they permitted with the "brave;"
When day by day the cleft between
Was wider made and plainer seen.

XLI.

And then with language stern and brief—
As emissary of the Chief—
Appeared a stoic savage face
At front of my abiding place,
Demanding of the French inmates
The stranger then within their gates.

XLII.

"For well we know," said he, "of fact,
'Twas of this man's unfriendly act
That our brave comrades, ten in all,
Of heartless foe were made to fall—
Bare one escaping, and he, who
Now recognizes their canoe
As of identity the same
With that in which the "pale-face" came—
The selfsame man who, once their prize,
Made safe escape before their eyes.

XLIII

Now mark ye of this grave demand,
Nor dare attempt to stay the hand
That springs the bow its shaft to speed
And cause the faithless heart to bleed.

XLIV.

Remember too, that of our tribe
The forest leaves are made describe
Our numbers, and of our prowess
The tribes around are made confess;
But of the French, though valiant too,
Of warriors have they but a few.

XLV.

Then hasten ye to give consent,
Or else to scorn our discontent,   •
That, of decision, we may know
If to regard you friend or foe."

XLVI.

Then spoke the chieftain of his clan:
And, cunningly, the shrewd Frenchman
Made bold to say in firm accent:
"Of your demand am I content
To give this man unto his fate
And of his crime to expiate—
Who of my kindred claimed to be,
Yet proves our common enemy.
Though of this life by you required
Allow me, of the end desired,
To arrange in full detail
A novel plan that cannot fail.

XLVII.

For yet three days of vengeance stayed
Trust to my care, nor be afraid

Lest he escape, which to secure,
I pledge my life that he appear
At place affixed and at the time
To expiate his awful crime.

XLVIII.

Within the time will I prepare
An ensign, and with colors rare,
A faithful likeness make thereon
To represent his heart of stone;
And to his bear back will I bind
The effigy, with will designed   .
To mark the place whereat converge
The life streams in their constant surge.

XLIX.

And ten best archers in the land
We'll station at a proper stand—
One to avenge each warrior slain—
To pierce the heart of Paul DePayne;
Who face toward the setting sun
Ten paces off, prepared to run,
Shall there await word of command
To save his life, if so he can.

L.

And archer with his bow and dart
Shall aim directly at the heart,
And each that strikes the bounds within
Shall beads and blanket from me win.

LI.

"Good. " saith the emissary brave:
"If through such ordeal he can save
His guilty life, we'll say 'tis charmed;
For since he ran away unharmed
From fire prepared for him a roast,
Some even now think him a ghost.
Though, hit or miss, I'm pledged with you
This novel plan to carry through
Remember, too, my words are deeds—
Also the BLANKETS and the BEADS."

LII.

When gone was he, the sly Frenchman
Revealed to me his cunning plan—
And this the plan to me revealed:
That ensign be, as well, a shield;
And that when fastened to my back
Of strength and firmness would not lack
To break the pointed arrowhead
And stay the missile at me sped.

LIII.

And of those archers did he know
Their great expertness with the bow,
And that the heart they'd pierce full well
As was the apple pierced by Tell.

LIV.

The time arrived, and—"one, two, three!"
Off went DePayne, straight as a bee.

LV.

"Snap" went ten bows with one accord,
And in the heart ten arrows stored;
But naught of Difference to DePaynne
Save impetus, his speed to gain.

LVI.

Then safe within designed retreat
Where, of appointment, was to meet
With aid and comfort from my friends—
Gun, ammunition, odds and ends—
I waited patiently till came
The messenger, and of the same
I learned that quiet was restored
And greatest friendship then assured:
Ten blankets and the beads, foretold,
Had settled for ten warriors bold.

LVII.

Before me lay the wilderness,
And of its wonders to possess
Was I an exile from the land
Whereof against me every hand.
As was, of old, with Adam's Cain
So was it then with Paul DePayne.

LVIII.

With friends reduced to, singly, one,
And that my ever trusted gun,
On it relied I for supplies
Of commissary, and likewise,
For all protection on my way

From Indians and from beasts of prey.

LIX.

No purpose had I, well defined,
Save former scenes to leave behind;
And cautiously, foes to avoid,
I westward then my course deployed.

LX.

One scene described, describes a score:
It was adventure o'er and o'er
With savage beasts and savage men,
As past the wigwam or the den
My course oft times was wont to stray—
Sometimes at night, sometimes by day.

LXI.

But I am dwelling far too long
'Pon incidents that ever throng
The mem'ries of that fearful time
And with my story bearing chime;
Though pardon me of one that bears
Upon the subject of our cares:
'Twas near a stream now known as Platte—
And ne'er was wilder scene than that.

LXII.

First came a deep and sullen roar,
As breakers on a distant shore;
And then, anon, as rushing storm
And thunderbolt, of fierce alarm,
There crashing came from o'er the plain

A rumbling, of still wilder strain.

LXIII.

And, casting far toward the north,
A dark cloud moved upon the earth,
And, with my camp direct in course,
Came with the speed of running horse.

LXIV.

Then closer drawn, and seen quite plain,
Were heads and horns, of furious mien;
And straight they came as arrow shoots,
A living sea of maddened brutes,
From whose escape did hope then seem
The phantom of a nightmare dream.

LXV.

But soon the first, with snort and bound,
Shied at my camp, to go around;
And, as the leader, so the herd:
Each that followed shied and veered
And left me fast within the flow
Of frantic, bellowing buffalo,
As island in a swollen stream
That threatens o'er its banks to teem.

LXVI.

A moment then an age appeared,
As onward moved the countless herd.
And when the train, at length, had passed,
With wonderment, I stood aghast
To see near by upon the plain

An Indian, and the brute he'd slain;
And yet another disengage
From out the herd, with frightful rage,
As, wounded with the spear or bow,
He sought the vanquishment of foe.

LXVII.

The Indian, though a stalwart "brave,"
To valor then discretion gave:
To run he thought the wiser plan,
And, face-about, the race began.
At running he was far from slow,
Though fleeter, still, the buffalo.

LXVIII.

'Twixt heels and horns the space declined
Till scarce a perch the horns behind.
Then leveled I my gun, with aim,
And, firing quick, brought down the game.

LXIX.

The red-man with amazement turned,
Whereof by him was I discerned—
Who then approached me and expressed
With signs and motions, suited best,
His gratitude for what I'd done:
Then pointed he toward the sun
And, of the gestures that he wrought,
Betokened of his favor bought.
As by that orb, its warmth, its light,
Proclaimed he of his heart aright

And, of true kindness more to own,
Made present of this little stone,
Whereof is sealed our friendship now--
Nor e'er was stronger plighted vow.

LXX.

And then, of gesture aptly made,
To follow him he kindly bade,
When o'er the plain, together, we
Strode onward to his rancheria,
Where found I, to my great relief,
My friend none other than the Chief,
Who of his subjects bade them go
And bring in camp the buffalo;
When, of the slain and roasted beast,
Was changed a funeral to a feast,
At which attended, with good cheer,
The tribe around, from far and near;
And of each honored royal guest
Had I of favor more attest.
Whereof, to me, it was quite plain
The Chieftain wished me to remain
With him. And, weary of my tramp,
Decided I there to encamp,
And duty, first, myself prescribe
To learn the language of the tribe.

LXXI.

Of this decision I essayed
With sign and grimace and cherade

To then make known unto my friend,
Who seemed at once to understand,
And, understanding, gave consent—
Inviting me into his tent.

LXXII.

He then, of gesture as foretold,
Me introduced to his household,
And thus of duties did assign:
His daughter, teacher—pupil, mine.

LXXIII.

Here, friends, forgive me of the pause,
For language fails me when of squaws
I would for charms invoke the muse:
Permit me time my words to choose.

LXXIV.

The hour is late, the fire burns low;
Now to my cavern shall I go,
And on the morrow, with God's will,
Return, my promise to fulfill.

INTERLUDE.

———•●•———

*O*F those encamped upon the hill,
Were Pete and Mike and Jack and Bill—
     All Crescent City men—
Besides a fifth one, called "The Squire,"*
Who busied was to stir the fire,
     And, of the meanwhile, then,
The others of opinion dared,
While yet the Squire was unprepared.

  'Twas not his tactics ever, though,
    To give opinion first;
  But when of others all to know
    His then he gave—reversed.

* See Note Three, Appendix.

Said Pete, "I think we're being bored;
Nor of the time can we afford
   To list the more from Paul DePayne."
"That's my opinion too," said Bill;
"I think he's giving us a fill
   Of words entirely vain
Of our purpose now to find
The old cabin where they mined
       In early day,
       Now lost, they say."
And Mike, with acquiescence, said:
"The old man has wheels in his head."

And Jack did of opinion join,
But said he had more time than coin
And, if the man cared to proceed,
It was us will to give him heed.

Again the fire gave forth its glow,
That on the curtained branches low,
Of tamarack and fir and spruce,
Was, of effulgence, made produce
The scenes with which, of fantacy,
The mind regales its imagery.

And then the Squire, with loaded pipe,
And self-prepared whereof to "swipe" *
The laurels that of fortune crown
The story-teller of renown,
        He thus began:
"Why! men," said he, "'tis my surprise
To hear you fellows speak thuswise
        About the man.

I've heard of Paul DePayne before,
And of his story am quite sure
That 'twill of purpose yet attain
To give us knowledge not in vain.

You may have heard the story, too,
Of how, upon Mount Siskiyou,
Was seen an ape, or spook, or tramp,
In region near to Happy Camp—*
        Some years gone by—
That was of stature taller than
The ordinary height of man—
Who fed on berries, roots and brouse,
Nor, of abode, had tent or house,
        And from whose eye
There gleamed the fierceness of the beast

---

  * Appropriated from local slang.
  † See Note Four, Appendix.

38

That, thwarted of voracious feast,
With sullenness, feigns to retire
Far in the jungle, to his lair;
Though loiters near his wanted prey
Till enemy hath gone away.

The same it is who now appears,
Divested of all former fears,
And selfishness, as well, subdued,
Lest others of his rights intrude—
The same it is, now Paul DePayne,
Renascent of himself again.

Then patiently let's bide with him,
And, though his story vague and dim
May seem to be of our design,
Let's to the sequel yet incline.

Though of the fate I most bewail,
The hermit's seeming endless tale
Gives me no chance to say a word—
Which, by the way, I think absurd.
Though of that comfort I'll forego,
To give the hermit ample show."

"Hurrah!" said Bill—"That's dealing fair."

And Pete thus said unto the Squire:
"That's better than we did expect,
And of its kindness will reflect
The honor of your name abroad"—
And then the party all hurrahed.

STORY RESUMED.

———•❖•———

I.

RETURNED am I, though poor, indeed,
Will be the story of your heed
Wherein of romance shall I make
The detail of a grave mistake:
For lesson first, that I then learned,
Was of a fact, quite well discerned,
That my fair tutress then installed—
Lolacondi, her name was called—
Had of design—to state in brief—
More than appointed of the Chief:
Seated on one hide, to suit,
She studied French and I, Piute;
And, aptly studious, 'twas not long,
Ere I was master of the tongue.

II.

Companionship, sometimes, enforced
By reason of all else divorced,
Remains intact when are reversed
The causes that inspired it first;
And, of the fancy thus betrayed,
Begets affection, true and staid.

III.

God said to Adam: "'Tis not well
To be alone." Then who dare tell
The soul that pineth for a mate
Its native longings to abate?

IV.

As of a stricken, helpless dove,
Perceived I of the artless love
That fettered Lolacondi's heart,
With wound from Cupid's aimless dart.
And may have she, as well, observed
The secret of my thoughts, reserved.

V.

Her form, at first, of comeliness,
Of faultless charm did soon possess.
Complexion, too, did I forget—
From duskiness changed to brunette.

VI.

Her smile became as rippling stream

With shade thereon and dappled gleam
Of sunshine peeping through the bower,
And in her trilling voice the power
That Cupid knows just how to wield
To pierce the heart, with arrow steeled.

VII.

With sparkling eyes and teeth of pearl,
And flowing hair, the Indian girl
Seemed then of rightfulness to claim
Of royal birth its proudest fame.

VIII.

And vaguely did I have in mind
The presence of two loves combined:
The first none other could displace—
The second, though, of hopeful grace.
One, of the brutal savage slain—
The other, of that blood whose stain
Had marked the fearful, heartless deed;
Nor of such rival could I heed.

IX.

Yet did I learn, to my regret—
Nor of consent from me to get—
That soon should be our wedding day,
When Chief, resigned, would give me sway.

X.

And of the stone the old Chief gave,
Was I informed its power to save

From dangers of the warrior foe—
(Though doubtfully of buffalo).
That of its charms were treasures found,
And friendships made of endless bound:
And of its favor more to lend,
The Chief did then on me depend.

XI.

And of its hist'ry, far remote,
'Twas found where western billows float;
Where even yet, 'tis said, are found
Upon the beach, and scattered round,
Some pebbles of the rarest sort;
The place is now known as Del Norte.*

XII.

Though, of this one, 'twill change its hue
From azure to the darkest blue,
And, of its changes, doth portend
Of fortune, to myself or friend.

XIII.

I've watched its change for many years,
Within my cave, with hopes and fears
Alternate with each change of hue;
But now 'tis of a darker blue
Than of that dreary time gone by,
And far more hopeful now am I

XIV.

Returning to the old Chief's lodge,
I'll now state of the artful dodge
That, of its planning, served me well
To make escape, yet not to tell
Of my unfaithfulness to him,
Or disapproval of his scheme
To wed me to the handsome squaw,
And thus make me his son-in-law;
And therewith give me of renown
The glory of a chieftain's crown.

XV.

Of this arrangement did I feign
Of all its honors to be vain;
And then, of prowess fair to show,
Claimed I the right, alone to go
Unto a distant warring tribe,
Whereof to me did they describe,
And bring as trophy to the bride,
From Chieftain's head the hair and hide.

XVI.

"That's good enough," the Chief rejoined;
And of the favor thus purloined,
My journey soon had I begun—
With face toward the setting sun.
They told me that ten sleeps away
I'd find the chieftain whom to slay.

XVII.

Though, many sleeps have I since had

And often times my poor heart sad,
And stricken low my soul with grief,
For Lolacondi and the Chief.

XVIII.

Yet onward came I, day by day,
As course of empire takes its way—
Across the "Rockies," then the plain,
Till reached a mountain range, again,
Where meet Sierra and Cascade;
And, as of difference to evade,
There meets in conclave with the two
Our grand old mountain, Siskiyou.*
Where, of the region, lakes abound,
And fish and game of plenty found;
And of the place decided I
There to remain—to live and die.

XIX.

Nor of my cherished talisman
Did I much heed or take in hand,
For since possession I had gained
Its color changeless had remained;
Though friendly were the tribes around,
And with them favor I had found.

—-o-—

XX.

Suffice it now to disengage

* See Note Six, Appendix.

From passing scenes, unto old age:

* * * * * * * *

Of childishness, perhaps, inclined,
The little stone then came in mind,
And finding it, perceived its blue;
And then athwart my mem'ry flew
The vision that me once impressed,
And still of counsel seemed: "Go west."

XXI.

Then on the mountain's rugged trend
I groped my way unto the end
Where saw I then, as now behold,
The waves upon the beach unfold
Against the rocky western shore—
Saw them splash and heard them roar.

XXII.

And then, of feebleness, I paused—
Old Time had claimed, of rightful cause,
The prize awaiting of his trust:
Then "earth to earth, and dust to dust"
Became the question of the hour—
Or else my body wolves devour.

XXIII.

And then decided I the plan—
As did behold my talisman,
That of true color did not lack,
And of such blue 'twas almost black—

Which gave me courage to proceed
With this my final earthly need.

XXIV.

My plan was to arrange a pile—
And, of convenience, did I smile
To find great logs of fir all heaped
And of their resin fully steeped;
And this should be my funeral pyre,
Wherein would kindle I the fire
At end remote from where I'd lie
When safe became my time to die.

XXV.

The time arrived, and, of the while,
Alighted I the funeral pile.
When, of the thirst that fever gave,
Of spring, near by, sought I to lave.

XXVI.

And shambling to its flowing brim,
With aching head and feeble limb,
There of my thirst did I then slake,
And from its bounty cupful take;
And feeling stronger, when returned,
Was glad the fire but feebly burned.

XXVII.

Then from my cup again I quaffed,
And, of a rashness, almost laughed
When reasoned I: "Of real truth,

Requited are from early youth
The pain, the anguish and the sigh,
Now thus, of ecstacy, to die."

XXVIII.

Then from the cup quaffed I again,
Though naught of fever or of pain
Disturbed the quiet of my soul.
"Old toper," said I: "Fill your bowl--
Drink, ye, to your heart's content!"
Then to the spring again I went,
With steady gait and form erect,
When from its depth did there reflect
A gleam as of the bright topaz,
Or sapphire of its lustre has,
And from it sparks of azure hue
Emitted were and flashing through
The limpid tide in miniature
That of my vision did allure;
And clasping it, the more to scan,
I found it was my talisman,
Which from my custody had slipped
And in the crystal fountain dipped.

XXIX.

With feeling, then, so much improved,
Was I of purpose aptly moved
The gruesome task yet to forego
As sexton—and as subject, too.

XXX.

And then, of bivouac to prepare,
Of lightness seemed its every care;
And 'neath the mantle of the night,
With scenes the rarest of delight
That e'er in fancy's roundelay
In noontide dream of summer's day
Inspired the finite mind with praise
To Nature's God, for all his ways,
Did dreams, elysian, throng my mind
With myriad raptures, all combined.

XXXI.

Then came the morn, with birds to sing,
And, from their dormer branches, spring
To catch the hapless little worm
That, "late from lodge," might homeward
        squirm—
And thus, for morsel delicate,
Rob home of parent, and a mate.
Yet from such gormand throats proceed
The songs that fairies deign to heed,
And so atone, with melody,
The evil--that of needs must be.

XXXII.

And when aroused, and on my feet,
Me old-time Nature seemed to greet
With radiant smile, as of my youth,
And cheering promise that, forsooth,

To castle-builder in the air
Would give the plummet, line and square.

XXXIII.

As youth inclines to sportiveness,
'Twas then my feeling to possess,
And, lest decorum should forget
And strive to turn a summerset,
My Bible opened I, to read.
Surprise! no glasses were of need.

XXXIV.

Then to the spring went I, again,
With bounding step and cheerful mien,
And, with ablutions and a sip,
Returned with hop and bound and skip,
Far unbecoming of my age;
And of my mind did thoughts engage
Of happy days yet far remote,
And o'er the fancy did I gloat
With boyish trust and confidence,
Until aroused to graver sense.

XXXV.

Succeeding days had change came o'er
Me as it had brief time before,
When chanced I in the spring to look :
And, as Narcissus, in the brook,
Was I portrayed with kind accent,
And on my features not a rent

Of Time's disturbing hand was there;
And raven were my locks of hair
As when in youthful age and prime.
For once defied, then, was old Time,
And in the swath his sickle bent,
And all his rancor vainly spent.

XXXVI.

But trying days then came, in turn,
And, of a scorching fever's burn,
Was I with fiercest torment scourged;
And of the pains within me merged,
Did seem to be, of greatest cause,
The soreness of my toothless jaws;
And of the virtues of the spring
As panacea for everything,
When of its service would engage,
Seemed only greater to enrage;
And, as of fretful teething child,
Was I, of torture, almost wild;
Till, strange to tell, though of a truth —
Discovery made—I had a tooth.
And filing, then, in quick relief,
Full set had gained in time quite brief.

XXXVII.

No fortune further to possess,
So came the need of needfulness;
And, of the passing hours to while,
Devices of the juvenile
Did I adopt, and with delight,

I sported with the top and kite,
As improvised with nimble hand
From best resources of command.

XXXVIII.

I'd laugh and skip and run and jump,
And play at "blindman" with a stump;
And other sports attempt to do
Wherein the game requires two.

XXXIX.

Then of a sudden happy thought,
That of my healing, overwrought—
With all its present seeming good—
I'd soon become "babe in the wood,"
I thus decided that 'twas time
For me to seek another clime
And from the tempting spring refrain
To take of pleasing draught again.

XL.

Yet down the rill, of source the same,
Descended I, in quest of game,
When—scene of wonder to behold!—
I found its bed was strewn with gold;
And of the bounty thus supplied,
I sought of plenty to provide.

XLI.

With speed then measured by my load,
My course, still westward, on I strode,

The mighty ocean's strand to reach;
Then southward turned along its beach—
With naught of interest on my way,
Till reached the San Francisco bay,
When fortune rare, then to avail,
Found vessel ready there to sail,
With products of the land well stored,
And destined for Atlantic board.

XLII

Then of three dreary months, or more,
When nearing of Atlantic shore—
And marvel I yet while I speak—
We sailed into the Chesapeake:
And to that land had I returned
That of my former self had spurned.

XLIII.

Though of my purpose, then in way,
Of greatest kindness to display
And, fortune then within command,
Give needy ones, with liberal hand,
It proper seemed that, ere to roam,
Ought charity begin at home.

XLIV.

But, oh! the thoughts within revived
Yet of my wand'rings not outlived.
The hand of art had wonders wrought,
And three score years of change had brought

New actors on the stage of life —
And naught remained of former strife.

XLV.

Of ruin was my birthplace marked,
Nor from its silence was there harked
Of voice from out its long decay
Save screeching of the startled jay
Within the bushes, rank and tall,
With rootlets clinging to the wall,
And, as from 'neath some mold'ring log,
The croaking of sequestered frog.

XLVI.

Thence to the spring my course did stray;
When, of the sultry summer's day
And mem'ries of the past so dear,
Twice grateful was I of its cheer.
Of all the scene it was least changed
From what it was of yore arranged.

XLVII.

Then stooped I, of the spring to drink,
And then upon the sward to sink,
Where, casting not too far around,
Returning childhood seemed profound.

XLVIII.

And, of the spell, did I give way
To slumber, as of childhood's day;

When saw I, in the cottage low,
My mother, rocking to and fro
Within her rustic easy chair,
As toyed she with my flaxen hair:
And father, too, of smile to win,
Would coddle me beneath the chin.

XLIX.

With brothers, sisters, and playmates,
Then hied we forth, to ride the gates,
And do of things, quite innocent,
That bad would be, save the intent.

L.

Distinctly then I heard: "Oh, Paul!"
And, answering to my mother's call,
I woke to consciousness again—
And sighed the fate of Paul DePayne.

LI.

Then of the schoolhouse, by the lane,
Sought I, but of seeking vain;
For naught of schoolhouse could be found,
Nor even LANE, upon the ground;
And of the grove, that once was there,
Of, even, stumps the place was bare;
Though scenes whereof I met that day
More sacred were that Lena Ray
Had, of her vision, known as well,
And often times to me would tell

Of those her pure heart loved the best—
And such I thought were truly blest.

LII.

My fame soon spread throughout the land—
Both of my wealth and liberal hand—
And of preferment was I, there,
With everyone, and with the fair
Was I at once a favored beau;
And, of my gallantry to show,
Was courteous, perhaps, to a fault;
And often times, of sad revolt
Was I, the stricken heart to see
That of requitement ne'er could be;
And, though regretful of the pain,
The pride of conquest made me vain.

LIII.

Yet, oft, when vict'ry seems to crown,
Is fickle smile changed to a frown:
The moth that flutters near the torch
Of pinion rarely fails to scorch.

LIV.

As in due season bird seeks mate,
So of myself, regenerate,
Was I then within the toil
That gladdens life or makes despoil.

LV.

Through it once my course had led,
And of its promptings had I wed;

And though its joys so soon were stilled,
The mission of a life fulfilled.
Though seemed it, then, the rule of fate
Of former things to duplicate;
And, of occasion opportune,
I met with Adaline McCune—
Than whom, of all the belles around,
None were of beauty so renowned—
Who with grace of form combined
A pure and highly cultured mind.

LVI.

Our meetings, though at first by chance,
Were not devoid of artful glance
Whereof the soul can mutely state
To other soul its love or hate.

LVII.

And, then, of meetings pre-arranged,
Were we from others more estranged,
Till of the presence scarce aware
Of more than two upon this sphere.

LVIII

Though rivaled was I, even then:
For who can tell of where, or when,
Since Adam courted mother Eve,
That such rare fortune did relieve,
And suitor of the fair assure,
Without a rival—one or more?

LIX.

Of purpose, now, I've none to state
More of this subject, delicate,
Than briefly to outline the way
Whereof deluded fancies stray
Into the realms of fond pursuit
To seek, perhaps, forbidden fruit.

LX.

Call it a conquest, if you will:
Of faithfulness then to fulfill
I sought the hand of Adaline,
And trustingly 'twas placed in mine;
When with forebodings gravely mixed
The signet ring I then affixed.

LXI.

Who that hath gained ambition's goal
E'er found the solace that, in whole,
Relieved the heart from further strain
Of anxiousness yet to attain
Some greater joy of its embrace?
Nay, even triumph brings menace.

LXII.

Then was I of a faltering mind;
Nor of consolement did I find
The time approaching near at hand
To take the Benedictine stand.

LXIII.

And in her presence once so dear,
I stood abashed as of the fear
Whereof the conscience, thus abused,
Confession makes when unaccused.
The truth had drawn upon my mind:
To her, and self, was I unkind—
In that the love to her I bore
Was less by far than that before.

LXIV.

So came the struggle of my life,
Compared with which all former strife—
Whereof to vanqish was I strong—
I reckoned not, as with that wrong
Of my own making; and that, too,
A wrong I could not then undo.

LXV.

Oft strayed I in the silent wood
To seek within its solitude
Consolement of my wretched state;
But Oh! the time then seemed too late:
No device of the mind could plan
To make me less the wretched man
That of my rashness was I made;
Nor less its scourgings to evade.

LXVI.

Resolved, at length, the spell to break—
Whatever course events might take—
I did of all my heart's design
Confession make to Adaline.

LXVII.

I told her of my purpose changed
And of affections disarranged;
And thought it better far that we
Be friends again, in "fancy free."

LXVIII.

Surprise to me!—her unsurprise.
Betokened of her calm, blue eyes,
And of demeanor so unchanged,
I saw at once her love estranged;
And thus she meekly answered me:
"How well our thoughts always agree.
I've thought as you have, Sir De Payne,
Though, of my feeling, did restrain
The truth as you have promptly told.
Oh, manly heart, how true, how bold!
Saved am I now from all regret,
That of life's fortunes we had met;
Excepting that for—well, you know."
And well did I—my rival beau.

LXIX.

Then happy was I of success,
Though chagrined that of worthiness
The minor share she gave to me.

How sensitive is vanity!

LXX.

Rebuked thus of my selfishness,
I thought upon the world's distress,
Whereof to me did fortune give
Much of its sorrows to relieve;
When in the hut, the lane, the street,
Its haggard face I strove to meet;
And fain my heart would, of the task,
Within the boundless duty bask.

LXXI.

Upon the street the half-clad child
I met, and parting, then it smiled.
And when I met, within the lane,
The beggar man who with his cane,
Could scarcely trudge his lonely way,
Happier was he of the day
Whereof our meeting to attain;
And happy too was Paul DePayne.

LXXII.

And in the hovel, at the door,
The lonely widow, aged and poor,
With gratitude my offering took;
When, of a wondering gaze to look,
She startled seemed, and then she said:
"Oh, image of the long past dead!—
Forgive me, Sir, yet do I hold
Your presence dearer than your gold.

Oh, tell me: Have I gone insane?
Are you the ghost of Paul DePayne--
My husband of so long ago,
Whose features yet so well I know?

LXXIII.

"Oh, Lena!" then I feebly gasped—
As of her bending form I clasped—
"Oh! Lena, dear, how can this be?"
But answer came not then to me.

LXXIV

Then followed weeks of patient care,
From doctors summoned, far and near,
And nurses—best within command—
While life and death strove, hand to hand:
Until, at length, the fevered brain
Once more of health and strength did gain:
And of her form, ematiate,
'Twas much improved from former state.

LXXV.

And, of her story, then I learned
Why, with the house, had she not burned
When in the flames so rudely cast,
As fuel added to the blast.

LXXVI.

One of the "braves"—indeed a brave—
Determined of our lives to save;

And, counsel failing to dissuade
The party from the fearful raid,
He cunningly devised to meet
And of their purpose cause defeat.

LXXVII.

And he it was who fettered me
And bound me, slackly, to the tree
With thong that, of my strength, would
      break—
Whereof, my freedom then to take,
And then, with seeming ruthless hand,
Did to my feet apply the brand,
That of mute language improvised,
With burning words, to make apprised
The object of his artful ruse,
Might deftly of my pinions loose.

LXXVIII.

And, in pursuit, all joined the chase,
Save he, who tarried to embrace
His purpose, then so opportune,
That executed was so soon
That scarcely failed he in the race
At once to gain the foremost place.

LXXIX.

Nor was he of the ten who paid
The measure of the crime portrayed,
But singled from the rest was he,

And from the deadly aim was free—
Whereof his guilty comrades fell—
And he the story left to tell.
No trace of me then to obtain,
So mourned as dead was Paul DePayne.

LXXX.

My wand'rings then to Lena told—
And of the spring and mine of gold—
Her smile assumed most rare delight,
As thus she said: "Oh, what a plight!
You're young and handsome still, but I
Am old enough that soon must die;
Though crowded in the present are
The pleasures of a life to share,
And restful in the grave I'll sleep
That of its care your vigils keep."

LXXXII.

"Dear Lena," then I gravely said:
"Think not to consort with the dead
Until we've tried a hopeful plan:"
Then told her of the talisman
And of its charms whereof should try
To make her even young as I.
Propitious, still, the little gem—
And sparkling as a diadem!

LXXXIII.

Proposal was, from me, command
To Lena, who, to understand,
In brief, the statement of my will,
Made it her pleasure to fulfill.

LXXXIV.

And, then, despite extreme old age,
Of task she did at once engage
To journey with me to the West;
And of the manner suited best,
I deemed 'twould be as first I went—
Direct across the continent—
And of equipment did provide
Convenient means whereof to ride;
Nor had we troubles on our way,
As journeyed on from day to day.

LXXXV.

Of incidents, I'll not intrude
Upon your time, save to allude
To one, as sequel now, in brief,
Of Lolacondi and the Chief.

LXXXVI.

We found their village, and I saw
And recognized the aged squaw:
'Twas Lolacondi, then most blind,
Who of my presence, though, divined;
And then of poise with cane to help,
She curtly said: "But, where's the scalp?"

LXXXVII.

The old Chief, though, had, long since, died,
And Lolacondi, ne'er a bride,
Was waiting still for my return—
Yet, of my faithlessness to learn.
Persuaded, though, she with us went
Our journey to the Occident.

LXXXVIII.

-— 0 —

Again arriving at the spring,
I found unchanged most everything,
And straightway, of its magic weal,
My patients there I sought to heal;
And counsel gave, lest of excess,
They'd drink to childish helplessness.

LXXXIX.

Then, with arrangements made for camp,
My leave I took whereof to tramp
In sportive way the region round,
For game, the rarest to be found—
Nor promise made when would return,
Save till my presence they discern.

XC.

And when of days thus gayly spent,
To camp again my course I bent,
And, of approach to near the spring,

I saw a child there, in a swing,
And swinging whom was Lena Ray,
As saw her on our wedding day.

XCI.

As Eden, of Creation morn,
With Eve its radiance to adorn,
So, of its glory to renew,
Was Eden then of Siskiyou.
'Twas Paradise indeed regained,
Nor greater joy could be attained.

XCII.

All nature did our purpose suit,
Nor knew we of forbidden fruit;
Nor yet came, as did with Eve,
The wily serpent to deceive
With age, the world had better grown,
And, of its sorrows, had we known
The bitterness that savors life—
Insipid, wholelely, without strife.

XCIII.

"But, Lena," said I, "whence the child?
And where the woman?" Then she smiled
And answering, said: "The twain are one.
And, oh!—we had the rarest fun
At romping, and at everything,
Till Lola tumbled in the spring.
I call her "Lola," now, that she

Is changed so much from used-to-be
That of her former self remain
But few the tokens now to gain;
And, as adopted child, I thought
To christen her anew we ought.

XCIV.

But now, dear Paul, I'm not amazed
That of her beauty you so praised:
When in transition from old age,
Did charms adorn that primal stage,
The first of blooming womanhood.
And seeing, then I understood
Why you were baffled, as expressed;
Though, of decision, am confessed—
And, of preferment, am I glad--
That doubtful promptings then you had.

XCV.

—o—-

Were Heaven on earth 'twould not suffice
To satisfy our craving eyes,
Nor of the longings would abate
Of finite mind, insatiate.
The more we gain of world's estate
The less its import do we rate.

XCVI.

The Eden of the wilderness
No longer did the charm possess

That of our restless souls could bind,
Or hope avert of joys to find
In other lands, and far away.
That of our cravings might allay.
Then blithly on our way we went,
Again toward the Orient.

XCVII.

With treasure, and with health and prime,
We journeyed on, yet of the time,
Or scenes we met upon the way
I'll not attempt now to portray,
Until within the borders of
The land of whence our primal love;
Wherein we met and recognized
Friends of the past, who, thus surprised,
Did scarcely of good faith express
Their credence of our truthfulness.

XCVIII.

It was a time when war again
Raged fearfully on land and main—
The second war twixt old England
And heroes of our patriot band.

XCIX.

Of patriotism, and for fame,
I sought to gain heroic name;
And of the chances to appear,
Upon the seas, as privateer,
Did then of purpose seem the best

For country and ambitious zest;
And, self-commissioned, Commodore,
I made equipments from my store
Of bounteous wealth, then of command,
And vessel well and ably manned.

C.

And when prepared were we to sail,
Vain were persuasions to prevail
With Lena to remain behind.
Said she: "Our fortunes are combined,
And braver far my heart will be
To share with you, upon the sea,
The greatest danger there in store
Than of your absence to deplore."

CI.

Then thought I of the magic stone,
And, of its gracious power to own,
I cast all fear at once aside
Whereof for Lena to provide,
Within the craft belligerent,
Arrangements aptly of intent,

CII.

And then, before the driving breeze,
We soon were on the great high seas,
Where drum and fife, with martial strain
Resounding on the placid main—
And not a foe within our sight—
'Twas pleasure thus on sea to fight;

And, with all peace and joy and health,
We were a floating commonwealth
That, of a thriving era had,
Was of its being truly glad.

CIII.

From day to day we onward sailed,
And south winds on our ship prevailed
To drive us to the leaward far,
With course toward the polar star;
When in the dreary nights that came,
The flicker of boreal flame,
As substitute for light of day,
Did poorly of the sun's delay
Give recompense, nor did preclude
The gelidness of latitude.

CIV.

And, on the frosty atmosphere,
Rang forth a warning, loud and clear:
"Boat, ahoy!"—from matin guard—
And fronting, on our ship's starboard,
Was flashed upon the lurid sea
The blazing of artillery.

CV.

And from that time dates there a blank:
'Twas said that from a drifting plank
Had I been rescued far at sea,
And lifeless seemed, at first, to be.

CVI.

More of events I never learned,
Save 'twas of vessel long returned
From out the war upon the main,
That did my helpless form regain.

CVII.

For years a prisoner, close confined,
Was I—of distracted mind—
From whence and when, till now, in vain
I've sought to find that spring again,
Whereof the gladness to recall
That Eden had before the fall."

SEQUEL.

I.

WHEN ceased the hermit to relate,
Descriptive of his past estate,
To his friends again he showed
The little stone, that fairly glowed
Then with the lustre of its hue

And purple scintillations threw
That pointed toward the western sea;
Then said the hermit: "Follow me."

II.

And staightway to the spring he led,
And to his comrades promply said:
"Someone indeed has here trespassed.
For since, of yore, my visit last,
That cabin on the hill was made."
"Lost Cabin Found!"—though much de-
  cayed.

III.

Then drank he till no longer old,
And two mules laden with the gold—
One fastened to the other's tail—
He drove them tandem on the trail.

IV.

Though of the party, who yet stayed.
They frolicked in the pleasant glade
And quaffed elixir from the spring,
And laughed and joked 'bout everything;
And, next—the saddest of regrets—
A fondness showed for cigarettes.

V.

Contriving, then, of ball and bat,
They played the game, "three-cornered-cat,'

And climbed the trees, the spring around,
Robbing birdsnests therein found—
Till tired, at length, there, of the play,
With sticks, for horses, rode away.

APPENDIX.

—◆—

NOTE 1. Refering to that most prolific incentive of wildly speculative mining excitements, "The Lost Cabin," the Del Norte Record,* dated Jan. 18th, 1883, says:

"Since the year 1852, various articles have appeared in print, not only in this State, but have found their way into the journals of the East, as well, concerning the far-famed stories of the "Lost Cabin." This much sought-for cabin has been located, according to the different tales concerning it, all the way from the Gulf Stream to the wilds of Montana and Colorado, and the first searching party started from various points along the coast.

* * * * * * * *

All those who were in Crescent City at an early date will recollect distinctly the excitement created by the report in circulation regarding this "Lost Cabin" and the time and money expended in searching for it. As the first person who went in search of it happened to be well known to us, having lived in our family for

---

* The DEL NORTE RECORD is a weekly newspaper published at Crescent City, California, by J. E. Eldredge, Esq., of whose favor the above facts and data are presented.

some time, and whose wife is now a member of the family, and as we consider that we are probably better posted in the matter than anyone now living, except it may be one person, who a number of years since was living in a lower county, we propose, briefly, to give our readers a statement of the facts as they actually occurred. In the year 1849, Col. Samuel C. Hall crossed the plains from Missouri to California, and drifting about with the tide of migration to different parts of the country in search of the precious metal, in the summer of 1852, found himself at Trinidad. While there, a party of three men came down from the mountains, one of whom, Vernile Thompson, was an old acquaintance of his from Missouri. After the usual greetings, questions were asked and answered in quick succession, and finally Thompson produced a large quantity of gold dust and confided to him the secret of where it had been found; saying at the same time that there was plenty left at the place where they had been mining. They had built a cabin which they left, and also their tools. They had three pack-mules pretty well loaded with dust, and with the usual reckless prodigality of miners in those days, thinking they had sufficent to last them for the remainder of their lives, never expected to return. They had left papers in the cabin with full instructions where the mines were located, should they ever wish to direct others to the place. Colonel Hall became greatly interested and having entire faith in their representations, obtained from them a diagram of the country which was reputed to be so rich, together with written directions how and where to find the cabin they had left but a short time before. They stated that the place was in hearing of the ocean's roar, but, as at that time but little exploring had been done on the northern coast, they could not give him the exact locality. The three men then left for the East. He immediately organized a small company and started in search of the rich diggings. They followed the directions as best they could, taking a northerly course and keeping within hearing of the ocean. They spent the summer in fruitless search, and by winter, the story having gradually leaked out, other parties started in pursuit of what had become known as the "Lost Cabin," meeting, however, with no better success. In the spring search was resumed, and the story having by this time been circulated that enormous wealth awaited the finder of the Lost Cabin, parties were formed and started out from different parts of the country, having but very little idea whether it was in California, Oregon or Washington Territory. Col. Hall, becoming discouraged, returned to his native State in 1854. In 1855 he again came to this country, with his family, and settled in Crescent City, where he remained for some years. He finally removed to Lakeport, and there met Thompson who had again come to California and settled in that place, and after a private interview with him, the Colonel could never again be induced to talk upon the subject of the Lost Cabin. It is supposed to be located somewhere near this place, and year after year it has been sought for, but no trace of the cabin ever having been discovered, many have supposed that the men who appeared at Trinidad with such large quantities of dust, had become possessed of their gold in other ways than by honest labor. However this may be, the above are the facts as they actually occurred concerning the Lost Cabin excitement in early times, a revival of which, has from time to time caused much excitement along the coast, and a great amount of hunting by those in search of immediate wealth."

From a long-ago intimate acquaintance of the author of this little volume with D. V. Thompson, (or Vernile Thompson, as above designated) it seems but just to offer a few words for the disengagement of sentiment questionable of the manner in which he and his associates became possessed of their treasure. Mr. Thompson was for many years, and, probably still is, a highly respected citizen of Lake county, California, where he has been honored with various offices of worth and confidence, and where his name was ever synonymous with that of strict integrity.

Assuming that the Lost Cabin story is not entirely a myth, it is doubtful if any other region could establish a more authoritative claim for its location than is presented in the foregoing account, for the westerly slope of the Siskiyou range, included principally in Del Norte county

NOTE 2. Relative to the prolonged and unaccounted-for absence of a miner from his cabin on French Hil, (subsequently found dead) the Crescent City News, dated Jan.25th, '95 says:

"It is said that of the eighteen disappearances around the French Hill country only one of the bodies has been found."

The preceding quotation would answer as a text upon which to found many speculations with respect to the mysterious disappearances from the region indicated. Such occurrences hav become so common, in fact, as to elicit, locally, only the stereotyped allusion: "Another French Hill victim." Many strange stories have obtained with reference to the misfortunes that have, or, peradventure, might have, befallen those who were thus seemingly spirited away, and yet no definite solution of the great problem has been reached. They simply become merged in obscurity, but whether of violence, of accident, or of self-volition, is a matter solely of conjecture; however, a sombre cloud of reproach has settled upon the shaggy brow of old French Hill, and, alas! the vaults of her native treasury

are less inviting to the miner and prospector
than if the spectre of the mysterious foe stalked
not her lonely caverns.

NOTE 3. The subject designated as the "Squire,"
at reference, page 35, is one of the distinguish-
ing featured of Crescent City, without whom
the place would greatly decline in its individu-
ality and become simply commonplace among
the towns along the Pacific sea-board. The
Squire is the essential oracle and weather-proph-
et of the town, and no one has yet attempted to
vanquish him in the relation of extraordinary
fish stories.

NOTE 4. A Del Nort Record correspondent,
writing from Happy Camp, Siskiyou county,
Jan. 2 , 1886, discourses as follows:

"I do not remember to have seen any reference to the 'Wild Man' which haunts this part
of the country, so I shall allude to him briefly.
Not a great while since, Mr. Jack Dover, one of
our most trustworty citizens, while hunting saw
an object standing one hundred and fifty yards
from him picking berries or tender shoots from
the bushes. The thing was of gigantic size—
about seven feet high—with a bull-dog head,
short ears and long hair; it was also furnished
with a beard, and was free from hiar on such
parts of its body as is common among men. Its
voice was shrill, or soprano, and very human,
like that or a woman in great fear. Mr. Dover
could not see its foot-prints as it walked on hard
soil. He aimed his gun at the animal, or whatever it is, several times, but because it was so
human would not shoot. The range of the curi-
osity is between Marble mountain and the vicinity of Happy Camp. A number of people have
seen it and all agree in their descriptions except
that some make it taller than others. It is ap-

parently herbiverous and makes winter quarters
in some of the caves of Marble mountain."

———

NOTE 5. One of the many attractive features
of the northern California coast is the renowned
Pebble Beach, in Del Norte county, near Crescent City. It has been a place of constant re-
sort since the earliest settlement of the place,
and it is known, even, that the aborigines had
esteemed of value some of the gems there found
long before their pale-faced brother came with
his trinkets and shekels to barter for the rare
and attractive jewels from the rude casket of
the guileless red man. But, still, the ebb and
flow of the tides continue to leave new and va-
ried attractions upon the beach, and the fasci-
nation for the pebble-seeker yet remains. The
pebbles found are principally agate and mocha-
stone, of divers colors and varying degrees of
brilliancy; though it is claimed that emeralds
and other high grade jewels have been discovered there. It is not extremely rare to find a
pebble of mutable color—the alterations being,
as supposed, influenced by the variations of
temperature and other meteorological phenom-
ena.

———

NOTE 6. The region of country briefly noted
at reference, page 45, as the abiding place of the
Hermit from early manhood till old and decrep-
it, has since become historic as the scene of the
Modoc War and location of the lava beds, where
Captain Jack, in his well-chosen natural fortifi-
cation, for months defied the attack of our gov-
ernment forces. The region is an exceedingly

high plateau, interspersed with lakes, hills and dales. The lakes are pure and limpid and abound with fish and fowl, and the hills and valleys are clad with the perennial bunch-grass, where, of the past, sported immense herds of wild animals. In its prestine splendor, it was indeed the Indian's paradise, and fairly typical of the happiest hunting ground that the exuberant fancy of the red man ever conceived. There, in immediate vicinity, presumably, upon the morning of Creation, met the three imposing mountain ranges: the Sierra Nevada, the Cascade and the Siskiyou—the latter of which, rectangular in extent, as compared with the two former, constitutes, in a manner, the natural, as well as the political, division of the states of California and Oregon, and approximate of whose easterly summit the Klamath river takes its source, from the lakes of that elevated region, suddenly precipitating its flow, in a raging cataract, to a level with the mountain range and thence girding it, latterally, to the sea.

www.ingramcontent.com/pod-product-compliance
Lightning Source LLC
Chambersburg PA
CBHW022009050726
47499CB00008BA/2698